Rick Boon is 31 years old. He lives in Yeovil, Somerset. He works as a postman and is a father to two boys, James and Tommy. He has a big passion for writing children's stories, taking inspiration from the natural world, as well as his own personal experiences.

Sid Gets a Job

Rick Boon

AUSTIN MACAULEY PUBLISHERS™
LONDON ★ CAMBRIDGE ★ NEW YORK ★ SHARJAH

Copyright © Rick Boon (2020)

A CIP catalogue record for this title is available from the British Library.

ISBN 9781528906548 (Paperback)
ISBN 9781528958929 (ePub e-book)

www.austinmacauley.com

First Published (2020)
Austin Macauley Publishers Ltd
25 Canada Square
Canary Wharf
London
E14 5LQ

For James and Tommy, my inspiration and my world.

I would like to thank Sandie Hindle and Dorg Gordon for their words of wisdom; without their help this book would not be the same.

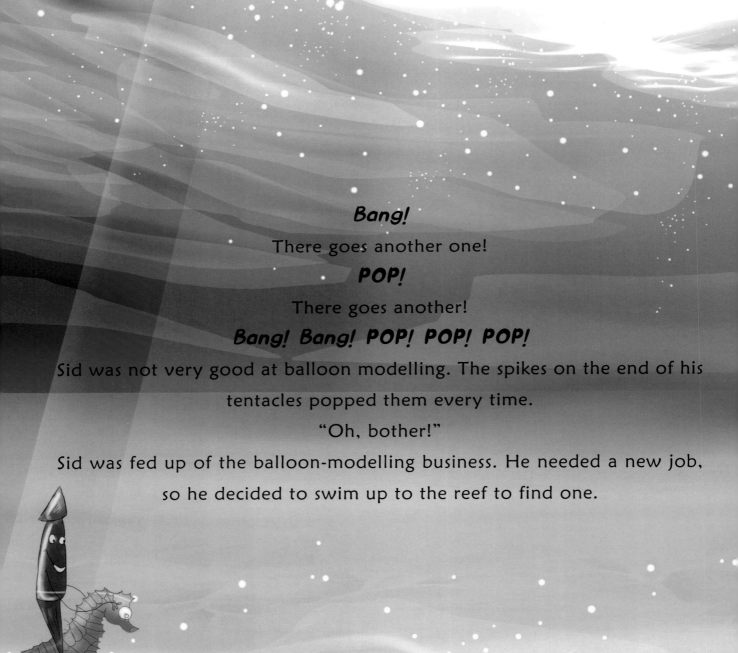

Bang!

There goes another one!

POP!

There goes another!

Bang! Bang! POP! POP! POP!

Sid was not very good at balloon modelling. The spikes on the end of his tentacles popped them every time.

"Oh, bother!"

Sid was fed up of the balloon-modelling business. He needed a new job, so he decided to swim up to the reef to find one.

On the way, he heard somebody whistling. It was Doug, the sea slug.

"What are you doing?" asked Sid curiously.

"I'm working," replied Doug. "I'm a postman. I deliver letters and parcels to everybody on the reef."

Sea slugs are slow. Very slow. It took Doug a long time to deliver all his mail.

"Can I help you deliver some of your letters?" asked Sid.

"That sounds like a plan!" smiled Doug as he handed over his postbag.

"I'll meet you at the Coral Café when you are finished. **Good luck!**"

Sid found that delivering letters and parcels underwater was extremely difficult. There were no street signs and no doors; no doors meant no letterboxes. Plus, the mail was wet! Nobody likes receiving wet mail! As for the parcels? Well, Sid wasn't having much luck with them either.

The rays got trays, the eels got wheels and the hake got a cake!

The cod got a rod, the jelly got a telly and the krill got a drill!

What a mix up!

"Oh, bother!

Eventually, Sid arrived at the Coral Café. Doug was waiting for him.

"Did you enjoy yourself? I saw you out on the reef, looking a bit lost..."

"No! I think I'll leave the post to you next time. But thank you for letting me help you."

After his disastrous attempt at delivering the mail, Sid decided to look for a different job. Further along the reef, there stood two loud crustaceans, shouting at the top of their voices.

"What are you doing?" asked Sid curiously.

"We are working," they replied. "We are market traders! The name is Bob Lobster – and this is Crabby Gabby!"

"You need to be very loud to be a market trader underwater; otherwise, nobody will hear you."

Visitors were arriving from the open ocean to look at the market stalls.
Soon, the reef was teaming with fish, turtles, rays and sharks – all looking
for a bargain.

Sid had an idea.

"Can I help you on your stall?"

"That sounds like a plan!" smiled Gabby. "We're off for our lunch.
Good luck!"

Sid found that market trading was very challenging underwater, especially
when he was trying to sell umbrellas! Nobody is going to want to buy an
umbrella when they live under the sea. Predictably,
Sid didn't sell a single one.

Sid found that market trading was very challenging underwater, especially
when he was trying to sell umbrellas! Nobody is going to want to buy an
umbrella when they live under the sea. Predictably,
Sid didn't sell a single one.

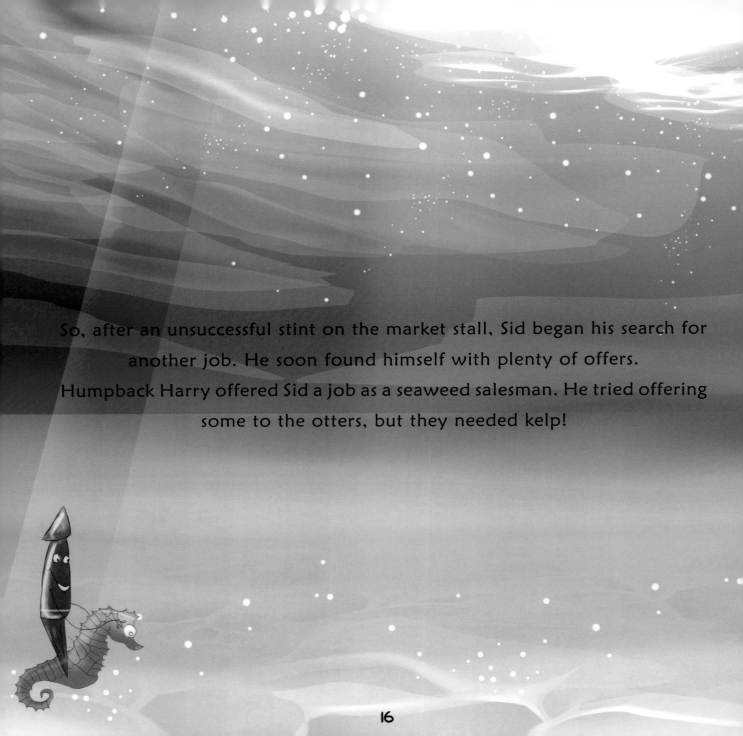

So, after an unsuccessful stint on the market stall, Sid began his search for another job. He soon found himself with plenty of offers.
Humpback Harry offered Sid a job as a seaweed salesman. He tried offering some to the otters, but they needed kelp!

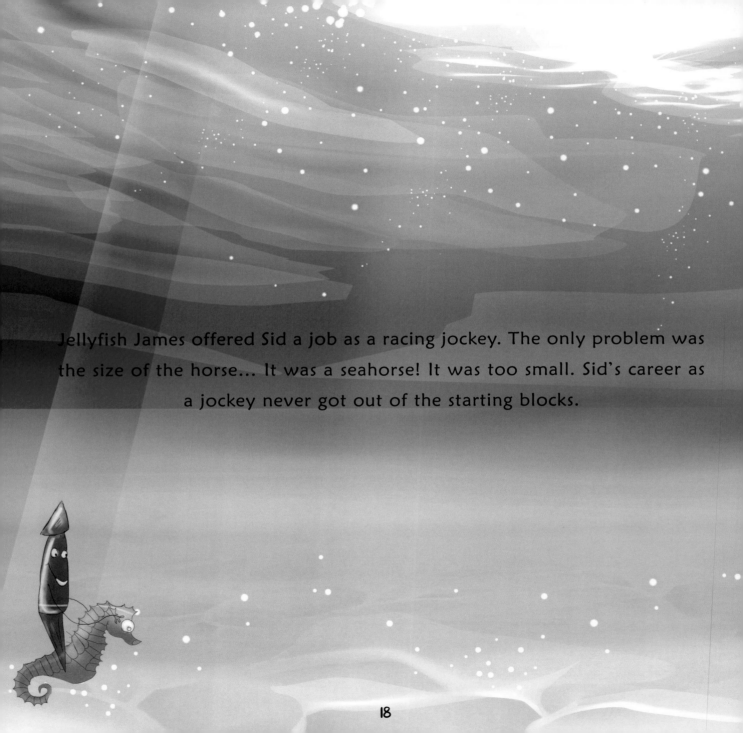

Jellyfish James offered Sid a job as a racing jockey. The only problem was the size of the horse... It was a seahorse! It was too small. Sid's career as a jockey never got out of the starting blocks.

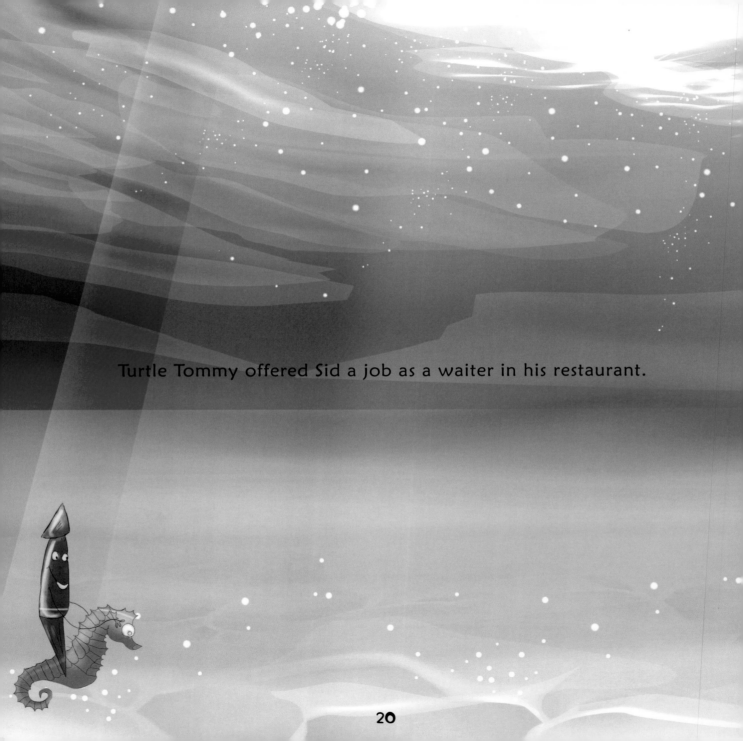

Turtle Tommy offered Sid a job as a waiter in his restaurant.

The only problem was that whenever the sperm whales turned up for their tea, they tried to eat him!

Every time Sid started a new job, something always went wrong.

"I'm never going to find a job, he thought."

Just then, Doug appeared. He had just finished his round and was about to head home when he saw Sid looking rather sad and fed up.

"Any luck with the job hunting?" he asked nicely.

"I have been everywhere on the reef today, but nothing has gone right. I have met some very friendly people, but their jobs are far more difficult than I ever imagined. I don't know what to do."

Then Doug had a fantastic idea. "I have the perfect job for you, Sid! Why don't you try having a go at being a tour guide? The reef is running short of them. You would be brilliant at that!"

Sid's face lit up. "What a good idea!"

He didn't have to blow up any balloons or post any letters. There were no umbrellas, he didn't have to ride any seahorses and he didn't have to persuade any otters to buy seaweed. It was the perfect job.

Sid is now a very successful tour guide on the reef. He has a job that he is good at and he is now the happiest squid in the sea. Sid may be a happy squid, but he still gets chased by sperm whales. Some things will never change!